Achoo!

Why Pollen Counts

by Shennen Bersani

"*Achoo! Achoo!*" Baby Bear sneezed. He rubbed his itchy, watery eyes, and sniffled his runny nose. Baby Bear lumbered out of his den into the warm, spring air. His fuzzy, black fur glistened in the morning dew. A coat of yellow dust covered the forest outside his home.

"*Yuck! Icky!* Why am I so sticky?" huffed Baby Bear. He stretched his sleepy muscles by rolling in a golden field of clover.

Valerie Vole poked her head out of her burrow. "You rubbed pine pollen on your fur," she said. "You have an allergy. *Achoo! Achoo!* I'm allergic to pollen too." Valerie sneezed as she scurried back underground.

"I don't like pollen!" bellowed Baby Bear as he scratched his face and rubbed his fur along the rough bark of a pine tree. "It's messy. It's itchy. It makes me—*ah, ah, a-choo*—sneeze! I wish there was no such thing as pollen."

"Pollen is more than sticky, yellow dust," soothed Momma Bear as she cleaned his fur. "The forest plants and animals need pollen. Some animals eat it and others move it around to help pollinate plants. Each plant makes its own type of pollen. Pollen comes in many shapes and colors. Some make you sneeze, but others don't."

"In the spring, I catch pollen in my web and eat it for dinner," said Sandy Spiderling as she swayed from a branch. "Some types of pollen are light and float in the air. The wind catches the pollen and carries it over far distances before it clings to my silk. Each night I roll up my web and eat what I've caught."

"Other types of pollen are heavier and cling to flowers," said Zoe Zebra Butterfly. She reached into a deep flower with her long proboscis. She slurped up the pollen inside. "Many insects eat pollen. Ant larvae, carpet beetles, wasps, and honeybees all think pollen is a tasty meal."

"Honeybees? I love sweet honey! But don't honeybees eat nectar?" Baby Bear asked.

"We do eat nectar," hummed Honey Bee. "But bees eat pollen, too. We have small baskets on our hind legs that we use to collect pollen. In the hive, we use pollen and nectar to make beebread. Our larvae grow strong eating the protein-rich beebread.

"Some animals—like butterflies, bats, bees, and hummingbirds—drink nectar from summer flowers. Pollen sticks to them as they travel from flower to flower. Everywhere they go, the pollen goes with them. After the flowers are pollinated, the plant can grow fruits, like apples and berries."

"*Achoo! Achoo!*" Baby Bear sneezed even louder. He fell backwards onto a hollow log. *Crash! Thump!* Lili Ladybug, still sleepy from long months of hibernation, flew out from the dusty cloud of pollen. She looked at the messy Baby Bear and laughed.

"I snack on pollen in the fall," Lili said, "when I can't find any aphids to eat. It has plenty of protein so I can hibernate in the winter."

Baby Bear shook himself off. "So Sandy eats pollen in the spring. Zoe and Honey Bee eat it in the summer. Lili eats it in the fall. Do any animals eat pollen in the winter?" asked Baby Bear.

"Yes," said Sammy Snow Owl. "Pollen floats high in a cloud. It clings to water, which freezes, forming ice crystals. As the ice crystals grow, they fall and form snowflakes. Some animals, like deer and wolves, eat snow in the winter."

"Who else eats snow?" asked Honey Bee.

"I do! I ate snow when I first came out of hibernation!" sang Baby Bear. "So I eat pollen, too! Pollen is part of honey, found in snow, and necessary for the growth of apples and berries. It's a food for some animals and helps plants grow into food for others. I guess I do like pollen after all."

For Creative Minds

Ah—Achoo! Understanding Allergies

Our bodies have all kinds of systems to keep us healthy. We have systems to help us breathe, see, taste, and many more. The immune system's job is to protect the body from sickness and infections. When you have a fever, your immune system is fighting to rid your body of a sickness. You might think of your immune system as a superhero that lets good cells in but fights to keep bad ones away.

Sometimes the immune system gets confused and thinks that some cells are bad that really aren't. Some of these confusing cells, called allergens, come from pollen, bee venom, mold, or even animal fur.

When the superhero immune system tries to prevent these allergens from getting into your body, you might have an allergic reaction. Like a fever, that is just the immune system's way of protecting the body.

Sometimes the allergic reaction is like the super hero going on the offensive . . . the immune system tries to push the allergens out of the body. A runny nose, watering eyes, vomiting, sneezing and coughing are all ways that the immune system tries to push the allergens out of the body. These reactions can be annoying and you might not feel well, but they won't hurt you.

If the super hero immune system goes on the defensive, it might shut down your throat or airways to keep the allergens from getting into your lungs. While that might keep the cells out of your lungs, it can also keep you from breathing. If this happens, you need to get medical help immediately.

Flower Parts

Pollen comes from flowers and is part of the life cycle in flowering plants. Flowers have many different parts that work together to make seeds that will grow into new plants. Match the description of the flower part to the image below.

1. The **stem** supports the flower's weight and connects it to other parts of the plant.

2. At the base of the flower are **sepals**. The sepals look like small green petals. They protect the flower bud before it opens.

3. The **petals** are often bright and colorful to attract pollinating insects and other animals.

4. In the middle of the petals is a single, vase-shaped **pistil**. Inside the pistil are several ovules. After pollination, the ovules will grow into seeds.

5. The pistil is surrounded by long, thin reeds called **stamens**. The stamens make pollen.

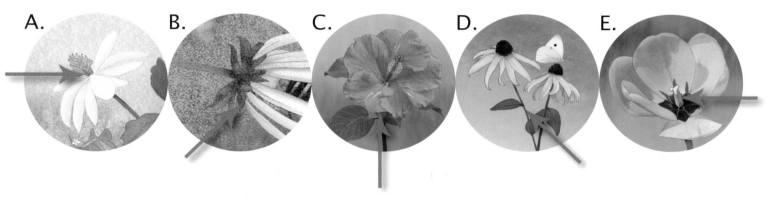

A.   B.   C.   D.   E.

Answers: 1-D, 2-B, 3-C, 4-E, 5-A

The Pollination Process

A flower produces pollen. Wind, water, or animals carry the pollen from one plant to another. If the pollen lands on a flower from the same species of plant, it joins with the ovule and becomes a seed.

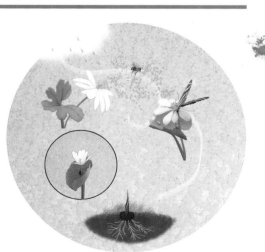

The seed needs space to grow. Wind, water, or animals carry it to a new place. The seed plants its roots and begins to sprout as a seedling.

As the seedling grows, it becomes a mature plant. This plant will soon produce flowers of its own.

Pollinator Matching

A pollinator is an animal that helps spread pollen from flower to flower. Some animals only like certain types of flowers. Read about the pollinators below and match each animal on the left to the flower they prefer on the right. Answers are below.

1.

Hawk moths are most active at dawn and dusk (crepuscular). They like to drink from blue or purple flowers.

A. honeysuckle

2.

Regal fritillary butterflies like flowers that grow in large clusters, giving them enough room to land. They prefer bright red, yellow, or orange flowers.

B. saguaro cactus flower

3.

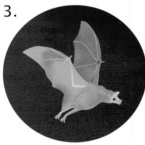

Lesser long-nosed bats sleep in the day and are active at night (nocturnal). They prefer white or pale flowers that open at night and are easy to see in the moonlight.

C. goldenrod

4.

Ruby-throated hummingbirds flap their wings 40-80 times each second. This helps them hover in place over a flower. They use their long beaks to reach into deep, funnel-shaped flowers and drink the nectar.

D. morning glory

5.

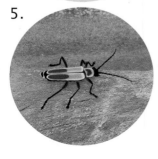

Soldier beetles are often found on yellow flowers. Yellow flowers are a source of food and a social meeting place for the beetles.

E. butterfly milkweed

Answers: 1-D, 2-E, 3-B, 4-A, 5-C.

Bees: The Great Pollinators

An ecosystem is made of all the living and nonliving things in an area. All of the things in an ecosystem are connected. Some species, called **keystone species**, play an important role in the life of the ecosystem. The keystone species helps other plants and animals live. If something happens to a keystone species, the whole ecosystem suffers. If the keystone species disappears, the ecosystem might even collapse.

Honeybees are a keystone species. When a honeybee lands on a flower, pollen sticks to her body. The bee carries this pollen to other flowers. By taking pollen from flower to flower, bees help the plants produce seeds. These seeds will grow into new plants. Honeybees pollinate more than 15% of all flowering plants. Without bees, these plants would have a hard time making seeds to grow new plants. Animals that eat plants (herbivores) and animals that eat both plants and animals (omnivores) depend on bees because they need new plants to eat. *Think about it:* If something harmed the bees, how would that affect the plants and animals that depend on bees?

People eat food from plants pollinated by bees. Bees help plants like almonds, apples, broccoli, carrots, chocolate, coffee, grapes, onions, peaches, tangerines, and tomatoes. Many people eat meat, and even our meat depends on bees. Cows, chickens, and other livestock eat plants so they can grow. Many of these plants are pollinated by bees. *Think about it:* If something harmed the bees, how would that affect people?

For the last ten years, many bees have been dying all around the world. In North America, a third of all honeybee colonies have disappeared. This is called Colony Collapse Disorder. Scientists are studying to find out why this is happening and how to stop it. For now, here are some things you can do to help honeybees:

1. Don't kill honeybees or hurt their hives. Most honeybees away from their hive will not sting unless you step on them or handle them roughly. Honeybees near the hive may sting if they think the hive is in danger.

2. Avoid putting pesticides or other chemicals on your lawn and in your garden.

3. Plant flowers! Find out what kinds of flowers grow best in your area. You can plant different kinds of flowers all year round. These flowers make nectar for honeybees to eat.

4. Bees need water to drink. Set up a small basin or birdbath filled with water. Place a few rocks in the basin so the bees have a dry place to land. This water will help bees and other thirsty animals.

My research for this book brought me outside, to living forests of New England, and inside, to quiet halls of the Harvard Museum of Natural History. I went to see live black bears in Lincoln, NH, at Clark's Trading Post; busy honeybees in their active hive at the Museum of Science, Boston, MA; and had close encounters with fluttering Zebra Longwing butterflies at Magic Wings Butterfly Conservatory in South Deerfield, MA; and at The Butterfly Place in Westford, MA. My heartfelt thanks to my supportive family . . . I love you all.—SB

Thanks to Dr. Alan Graham, Curator of Paleobotany & Palynology at Missouri Botanical Garden's Center for Conservation and Sustainable Development, for reviewing the accuracy of the information in this book.

Library of Congress Cataloging-in-Publication Data

Bersani, Shennen, author, illustrator.
 Achoo! : why pollen counts / by Shennen Bersani.
  pages cm
 Summary: Baby Bear does not like pollen, which sticks to his fur and makes him sneeze, but insects and other animals tell him how important pollen is, even for him. Includes an activity and facts about allergies, flowers, and pollinators.
 ISBN 978-1-62855-550-9 (English hardcover) -- ISBN 978-1-62855-559-2 (English pbk.) -- ISBN 978-1-62855-577-6 (English downloadable ebook) -- ISBN 978-1-62855-595-0 (English interactive dual-language ebook) -- ISBN 978-1-62855-568-4 (Spanish pbk.) -- ISBN 978-1-62855-586-8 (Spanish downloadable ebook) -- ISBN 978-1-62855-604-9 (English interactive dual-language ebook) [1. Pollen--Fiction. 2. Allergy--Fiction. 3. Bears--Fiction. 4. Animals--Fiction. 5. Pollination--Fiction.] I. Title.
 PZ7.B467Ach 2015
 [E]--dc23
        2014037343

Translated into Spanish: ¡Achíss! La importancia del polen

Lexile® Level: 670L
key phrases for educators: adaptations, allergies, basic needs, keystone species (honeybees), plant life cycle, plant parts, pollen, and pollinators

Bibliography:

Carlton, Marc. "How Insects Feed From Flowers." The Pollinator Garden. Updated 2011. Web. Accessed February 2014.
Cochran, Sylvia. "What is Pine Pollen." Garden Guides. Web. Accessed February 2014.
Colorado State University. "Amount of Dust, Pollen Matters for Cloud Precipitation, Climate Change." Science Daily. Published July 2010. Web. Accessed February 2014.
Dunn, Rob. "Pollen." National Geographic. Published December 2009. Web. Accessed August 2014.
Eggs, Benjamin. "Herbivory in Spiders: The Importance of Pollen for Orb-Weavers." PLoS ONE. Published November 2013. Web. Accessed March 2014.
"How Pollen Allergies Affect You and Your Pets." Updated March 2014. Web. Accessed April 2014.
Jolivet, Pierre. Interrelationship between Insects and Plants. CRC Press, 1998. Print.
Sanders, Kevin. "Bearman's Guide to the Bears of Yellowstone Park." Web. Accessed February 2014.
"What Bees Eat." College of Agriculture and Life Sciences, University of Arizona. Web. Accessed February 2014.
"Why We Need Bees." National Resource Defense Council. March 2011. Web. Accessed February 2014.

Manufactured in China, January, 2015
This product conforms to CPSIA 2008
First Printing

Arbordale Publishing
Mt. Pleasant, SC 29464
www.ArbordalePublishing.com